PEST friends

More Maxine and Minnie stories

Kind of Twins
Friends Forever

PEST
friends

by Pippa Goodhart

illustrated by Ailie Busby

EGMONT

For pest friends,
Anna G. and Anna C.

First published in Great Britain 1997
by Egmont Books Limited
239 Kensington High Street, London W8 6SA

Text copyright © 1997 Pippa Goodhart
Illustrations copyright © 2003 Ailie Busby
Cover illustration copyright © 1999 Ailie Busby

The moral rights of the author and illustrator
have been asserted.

ISBN 1 4052 0409 5

1 3 5 7 9 10 8 6 4 2

A CIP catalogue record for this title
is available from the British Library

Printed in Great Britain
by Cox & Wyman Ltd, Reading, Berkshire

Contents

1 Making friends!

Maxine and Minnie were best friends, but you might wonder why. They were not at all like each other.

Maxine was big and loud and funny. She had green eyes and a wide smile. She had a wild frizz of orange hair that looked like a burning bonfire. Maxine liked to be colourful. If she couldn't find ribbons to go in her hair, then she used coloured clothes-pegs. Maxine liked to be noticed. She had pink, spotty leggings and a dress that sparkled with tiny

mirrors and jingled with bells.

Minnie was different. Minnie was small and she was shy. She wore a plain hairband and ordinary school clothes and hoped that nobody would notice her.

When they were side by side, Maxine and Minnie looked as if they were the same height, but that was because Maxine was in a wheelchair and sitting down. They really were different in almost every way. So, why were they friends? It was simple. They both needed a friend at the same time.

The day before Minnie arrived in Mrs Dobbs' class was the day that Maxine fell out with her old friends. All the girls in

Mrs Dobbs' class had been collecting animals that came free in packets of Puff Pops. They were called Little Cutey Zoo Animals and Maxine didn't like them. She thought that they were just boring lumps of plastic with big eyes and soppy smiles.

'Why don't you collect real animals?' Maxine asked. 'Make a real little zoo?'

'Because you can't get real little snakes and monkeys, stupid!' they said. So Maxine made a real little zoo just to show them. She lifted stones at the edge of the playground and found a wriggly pink worm-snake and a spider monkey. She found two juicy snails too. Maxine put her animals into her empty lunch box and showed it to the others. 'Here's my real zoo,' she told them. 'Do you like it?'

One girl screamed and ran away.

A boy said 'Yuk,' and poked at the worm.

'Don't! You'll hurt him!' said Maxine.

The girl who had run away told Mrs Dobbs about Maxine's zoo. Maxine got told off, and that is why Maxine needed a new friend on the day that Minnie came to the school.

Minnie needed a friend because she was new. She had only moved house the day before and she didn't know anyone.

Being new is always hard, but it was extra hard for Minnie because she was shy. She had to stand at the front of the class feeling all hot and pink. She tried to hide behind Mrs Dobbs, but Mrs Dobbs pushed her forward and said, 'Everybody, this is Minnie Brown. Today is her first day in our class and I would like one of you to sit with her and look after her.'

Minnie wanted very much to find a real friend. She wanted the sort of friend she could invite home for tea. She

wanted the sort of friend she could stay the night with. But all the children in Mrs Dobbs' class knew each other already. Minnie thought, none of them will want to bother with me. But then she heard a voice from the back of the class.

'Me! Oh, please, me!' said the voice. 'I want to look after her!' Minnie looked across to where the voice had come from and she saw a girl with orange hair and a big smile.

But Mrs Dobbs shook her head. 'I'm sorry, Maxine,' she said. 'You can show Minnie around at playtime, but I'm afraid that there just isn't room for her to sit with you in class.'

And Minnie looked and saw that it was true. Maxine sat at a table all by herself. Her wheelchair didn't leave enough room for another chair to fit in beside her. Mrs Dobbs began finding another place for Minnie to sit, but Minnie didn't want that. She wanted to be with Maxine. Minnie tugged at Mrs Dobbs' sleeve. Mrs Dobbs looked down at her. Minnie went even pinker. She pointed towards the book corner where there was a little stool. 'Please,' she whispered, 'could I use that?'

'Well, yes, I suppose you could,' agreed Mrs Dobbs. 'But it is rather low.'

The stool was low. It was quite a lot lower than Maxine's chair, but it fitted beside it very well. And Minnie smiled up

at Maxine and Maxine smiled down at Minnie, and that had been the start of their friendship.

At playtime Maxine talked a lot and Minnie talked a little.

'Where do you live?' asked Maxine. 'Have you got any brothers and sisters? Have you got animals? Do you like cheese?'

Minnie wasn't sure what to answer first. 'I've just moved to Church Street,' she said in her quiet voice. 'Number 21.'

Maxine punched her fists into the air and shouted, 'Brilliant! Double brilliant! You're next door to me! I saw the van arriving with all your stuff yesterday, but you must have moved in when I was at school. We'll be able to see each other whenever we want!'

Minnie thought about the house next door. She remembered seeing toys in the garden and a very long line of washing. 'Are there lots of you?' she asked.

'Yes,' said Maxine. 'There's Mum and Dad and me and Darrel and Ben and Sarah and Baby Bobo and Hamish.'

'Eight people!' said Minnie.

'Not eight,' said Maxine. 'Only seven. Hamish is a dog.'

'Seven is still a lot!' said Minnie. 'I've only got Mum and me.' Then she thought of something. 'Why did you ask me about cheese?'

'Because,' said Maxine, 'your name is Minnie like Minnie Mouse, and your surname is Brown like the Little Brown Mouse, and because you look like a mouse. I think that you might actually be a mouse. If you like cheese, that would prove it.'

Minnie thought about what Maxine had said. It was true that she was mousey. She had mousey brown hair and a mousey pointed nose. She was mousey shy.

Once at Granny's house she had seen a mouse close up. Minnie had sat in Granny's chair and stayed so still for so long that a little mouse had come and eaten crumbs off the floor and never noticed her. Minnie had liked that. She liked mice and would quite like to be one.

'I do like cheese,' she told Maxine. 'Even better than chocolate biscuits.'

'Well that proves it then!' said Maxine. 'You must be a mouse. All you need to be a proper mouse is a tail. I'll make you one.'

'Thanks,' said Minnie. She wanted to make something for Maxine too, but what? 'What would you be if you could be something different?' she asked Maxine.

'You mean if I wasn't just a person?' asked Maxine.

'Yes,' said Minnie.

Maxine thought for a moment. 'I'd be a machine,' she said. 'I would be Maxine the Amazing Machine that could race faster than a train and make you anything you wanted. And I'd be able to fly. I'd love to fly.'

'Then you need wings,' said Minnie.

It rained that afternoon and so there was Wet Play when you could make things. Maxine found a long brown sock in the ragbag. She stuffed it with old tights and sewed it up. 'There we are,' she said. 'A mouse tail!' She tucked it into the top of Minnie's skirt.

Minnie wiggled her bottom and swung the tail with her hand. It felt nice. 'Thanks!' she said.

But Maxine hadn't finished.

'It's a bit of a boring tail,' she said. She took a pink spotty ribbon out of her hair and tied a bow near the bottom of the tail.

'That's better!' she said.

Minnie made Maxine some wings. Although aeroplane wings would have been right for most flying machines, Minnie didn't think they would be right for Maxine. They would have stuck out sideways and got in the way, and they would have been dull. So Minnie made fairy wings. They were made out of cardboard and stuck all over with bright shiny bits and pieces. Minnie took off her hair-band and used it like a big elastic band to tie the wings over the handles at the back of Maxine's wheelchair.

'The only trouble is that the wings are behind me and I can't see them!' said Maxine.

'It's the same with my tail!' said Minnie.

Mrs Dobbs came to see what they had been making.

'A mouse tail,' said Maxine. 'I made it for Minnie.'

'I made wings for Maxine,' said Minnie.

Mrs Dobbs laughed. 'Well it looks to me as though you've also been making friends!' she said.

Maxine and Minnie looked at each other. They smiled.

'Come to tea at my house?' said Maxine.

'Yes, please,' said Minnie.

2 Feeling scary

Minnie didn't go to Maxine's house just for tea. She went to Maxine's house for tea and the night and most of the next day. That was because her mum had to visit Minnie's granny in hospital a long way away.

It was noisy at Maxine's house because she had so many brothers and sisters. Maxine's dad showed the rest of them how to play a monsters game. You had to draw a monster head at the top of a bit of paper and then fold it over and pass it on. Then you drew a monster body and folded that over and passed it on again for the next person to draw the legs. When all that was done you opened up the paper to see the whole monster. Some of them were very funny.

It was a different sort of evening from the quiet ones that Minnie was used to at home with Mum. She felt rather shy and didn't say much.

Then it was bedtime and Minnie shared Maxine's bedroom. At home Minnie only shared her bedroom with

Wild Thing. Wild Thing was a soft toy. He had horns and big teeth, but he smiled in a friendly way.

Minnie had brought Wild Thing with her to Maxine's house, but she hadn't taken him out of her bag.

It was after nine o'clock and Maxine and Minnie were still chatting when Maxine's mum knocked on the door.

'Are you girls still awake?' she said. 'It's very late.'

'But we're not tired,' said Maxine. 'It would be a waste of being together just to sleep!'

Maxine's mum laughed. 'I know you, Maxine Higgins. You'll turn into Mad Max the Monster by the end of tomorrow unless you get some sleep now.'

'But we're not tired!' said Maxine. 'I know,' she said, 'why don't you tell us a story about a mad monster? Go on,

Mum! It'll make us sleepy!'

'Really?' asked Maxine's mum. 'Are you sure that you want a scary one?'

'Yes!' said Maxine.

'What about you, Minnie?' asked Maxine's mum. 'Do you like scary stories?'

Minnie didn't know whether she liked them or not. She had never heard one. But Maxine wanted one, so Minnie nodded.

'Right,' said Maxine's mum. 'Here we go . . .

'One dark, stormy night, a man got

18

lost in a wood. He walked and he walked, looking for a path that would lead him home. After some time he came

across a big house all on its own, deep in the wood. There were no lights on, but the man was tired and desperate for shelter. He knocked on the door, but nobody came. So the man just pushed the door open and went in.

'The door slammed shut behind him. Inside the house the man found a bed and he got into it and went to sleep. But in the middle of the night, he suddenly woke up!'

Minnie pulled her sleeping-bag tight round her. Maxine's mum went on: 'It was still dark and the man couldn't see anything. He could hear something, though. He could hear thump, thump, thump!'

Minnie bit hard on a corner of her sleeping-bag.

'Go on, Mum!' said Maxine.

'The man called out, "Who's there?"

20

but there was no reply. The only sound now was the sound of the man's heart thumping with fear.'

'I bet it was just his heart noise all along!' said Maxine.

'I hope so,' said Minnie in a little voice.

Maxine's mum held up a finger. 'That's just what the man began to think,' she said. 'He told himself, "There's nobody there! I'll put on a light and show myself that there's nobody there." So he reached for his torch. And . . .' Maxine's mum bent down and whispered the next bit. 'He felt something, but the something wasn't a torch. It was a hand! A hairy hand with claws! And the hand gave the man his torch!'

'Oh!' squeaked Minnie. She hardly dared ask, but she wanted to know. 'Did he turn on the torch and look?'

'I would have!' said Maxine.

Her mum laughed. 'I've no idea! But I do know that it's time that you two got some sleep. Goodnight!'

'Goodnight,' said Maxine.

'Shall we talk a bit more?' said Minnie. She wasn't sure that she dared go to sleep now. With the lights out, she couldn't help thinking about the man asleep in the house in the woods hearing . . .

'What was that?' squeaked Minnie.

'What was what?' asked Maxine in a sleepy voice.

'That noise by the window!' said Minnie.

Maxine yawned. 'That's just Sooty the cat from next door. He always jumps on to my windowsill.'

'Oh,' said Minnie. She had forgotten that she was in a downstairs bedroom. A car drove past and its lights lit up the shape of the black cat on the windowsill. Like a witch's cat, thought Minnie. The

lights came right inside the room and
made moving blobby shapes that slid
over the ceiling and walls. Like ghosts,
thought Minnie.

She felt all shivery. Minnie knew that
she wasn't going to get to sleep without
Wild Thing to cuddle, and he was still in
her bag on the other side of the room.

Minnie wriggled out of bed and felt her way across the room. She put her hand where she thought her bag was, and she touched something hairy and hot.

'Oh!' screamed Minnie.

'Ow!' shouted the hot, hairy thing.

'Why are you poking me?' asked Maxine.

'Sorry,' said Minnie. 'I thought you were a monster.'

Minnie found Wild Thing and climbed back into her sleeping-bag. 'I keep thinking about monsters,' she said.

'But there are no such things!' said Maxine.

'I know,' said Minnie.

At home, if Minnie couldn't get to sleep, Mum would come and turn over Minnie's pillow and say, 'Try and think about something nice.'

'I think I'll have to think about nice monsters,' said Minnie. 'Wild Thing is

24

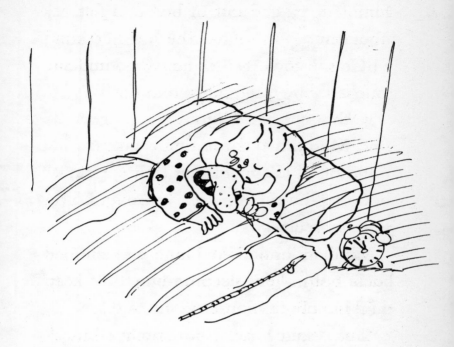

nice. He's nice-funny.'

'If you want something funny to think about, then think of a way we could scare my mum tomorrow!' said Maxine. 'It would serve her right for scaring you with her story!'

Minnie thought. Would it be a nice thing to think about? It would just be for fun! 'All right,' said Minnie. 'I'll think about that.'

'Good,' yawned Maxine. 'Goodnight.'

'I've thought of how to scare your mum!' said Minnie next morning. 'The scariest thing of all last night was feeling you, all hot and hairy! So, let's make a hairy-monster feely-box!'

'Brilliant!' said Maxine.

'But I'm not sure how to do it,' said Minnie.

'Easy,' said Maxine. 'Follow me!'

Maxine rummaged around and found an empty shoe box, bits of wool, an old rubber glove, sand, paper, pens, glue and scissors, a bit of sponge and two grapes. She and Minnie shut themselves in Maxine's bedroom. Maxine's mum could hear chatter and giggles through the door as she cooked lunch in the kitchen.

Then Maxine and Minnie came out of the room. 'We've made a present for you, Mum,' said Maxine.

'It's not my birthday!' said Maxine's mum. 'What have I done to deserve a present?'

'Scared Minnie!' said Maxine. 'Go on, open it!'

Maxine's mum slowly peeled back the wrapping-paper.

'Oh, no!' she said. The shoe box had been turned into a hairy monster head with an enormous mouth hole with dangling paper teeth hiding the inside of the mouth.

'Put your hand in!' said Maxine. 'Then you'll feel what it's eaten for its lunch!'

Minnie squeezed her hands tightly together and Maxine leaned forward to watch as slowly, very slowly, Maxine's mum put her hand into the monster's mouth. She reached inside and made an awful face. 'Yuk!' she said. 'It feels like a dead hand!' Then Maxine's mum made an even worse face, 'And squashy brains and two eyeballs! Euch!'

Maxine and Minnie laughed so much that it hurt. Maxine's mum went on making terrible faces and Minnie began to feel sorry for her. 'It's nothing really horrible,' she told her. 'The hand is just a

rubber glove with sand in it and the brains are a wet sponge.'

'But what about the eyeballs?' asked Mum. 'They feel so real!'

'Just grapes!' laughed Minnie.

'Well, thank goodness for that!' said Maxine's mum. 'Now, would you call Dad and the others for lunch? It's all ready.'

'What are we having?' asked Maxine. 'I'm starving!'

Maxine's mum made a witchy face. 'It's worms in blood sauce!' she said.

Minnie looked on the table and saw worms in blood sauce. 'I'm not very hungry,' she said.

Maxine laughed. 'It's only spaghetti in tomato sauce, you twit!'

'Oh, good,' said Minnie. She put a hand up to hide a yawn. Being at Maxine's was fun, but Minnie was looking forward to a quiet evening at home with just Mum and Wild Thing.

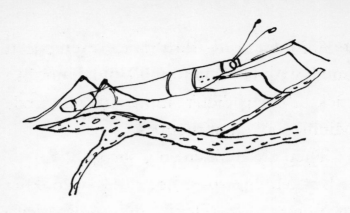

3 Butterfly fingers

'What's brown and sticky?' asked Maxine.

Minnie thought of mud or chocolate fudge or something worse.

'Shall I tell you?' asked Maxine.

'Yes,' said Minnie.

'Stick insects!' said Maxine. 'Stick insects are brown and stick insects look like sticks, so they're sticky! Look in there!' Maxine pointed into the glass tank that Mrs Dobbs had brought into class. The tank looked as though it had just twigs and leaves in it, but now

Minnie could see that there were insects on the twigs. They really were just like sticks. They didn't move at all while Minnie looked at them.

'They are a bit creepy,' she said.

But Minnie soon got used to looking at insects. Mrs Dobbs did insects with them all week. She told them that they were going to do an assembly on insects for the whole school. They wrote insect poems and made insect pictures. They made dancing spiders out of egg-box humps and pipe-cleaners and elastic. They did creeping and crawling in PE.

By the end of the week Minnie quite liked insects. She didn't scream when Maxine pretended that she could see an earwig in her ear and she hardly felt tickly at all when Mrs Dobbs talked about fleas. She was really looking forward to the assembly. Mums and dads were allowed to come to it.

'And,' Mrs Dobbs told them, 'to make it really fun I thought we might all dress up as insects and I will give a small prize for the best costume!'

That set the class buzzing with excitement.

'Brilliant!' shouted Maxine. Then she turned to Minnie. 'Let's win!'

'Come to my house tonight, and we'll think what to wear,' said Minnie.

So Maxine went to Minnie's house for tea. Minnie's mum ate tea with them.

'What have you two been doing at school today?' she asked.

'Talking about these!' said Maxine, and she flicked something small and black and leggy across the table.

'Eeek!' squeaked Minnie's mum. She jumped up from her chair. 'Take it away!' she said.

'But it isn't a *real* spider!' said Maxine.
'It's only the top from my tomato! It's a
good trick, isn't it?'

'Mm,' said Minnie's mum, and she sat
down but she didn't laugh.

'Sorry,' said Maxine. *Her* mum would
have thought it was funny!

Minnie told Mum about the special
assembly and the prize for the best insect
costume. 'Oh, and I almost forgot, Mum,
Mrs Dobbs says can you play the piano

for us? I told her that you could play! Nobody else has a mum who can do it!'

'Oh, I don't know,' said Minnie's mum. 'I've never played the piano in front of other people!'

'But I told Mrs Dobbs that you would!' said Minnie. 'Oh, please, Mum! She's given me the music and everything!'

'Oh dear,' said Minnie's mum. 'Well, I suppose I shall have to then!'

After tea Maxine and Minnie thought about their insect costumes. They looked at pictures of insects in books.

'Ladybirds are pretty,' said Minnie.

'But I bet everybody will choose ladybirds,' said Maxine. 'We want to be something different from all the others. I'd like to be a flea, but in all the pictures of fleas you can see right through them! It's going to be hard to really look like an insect.'

'But Mrs Dobbs didn't say we had to look like *real* insects!' said Minnie. 'Why don't we make up our own sort of insects? Then nobody can say that we've got it wrong!'

'Brilliant!' said Maxine. 'We can be Insects From Outer Space!'

Maxine and Minnie got out glue and scissors and paper and pens and Minnie's mum's ragbag.

'Put newspaper on the table, please,' said Minnie's mum. 'And wear aprons.'

Then they set to work.

'Insects have six legs!' said Minnie, so they made an extra pair of legs each.

'And they can have eyes on long things coming out of their heads!' said Maxine.

'Antennae,' said Minnie. So they made some of those.

'We can have funny noses too,' said Minnie. 'We can have anything we like because we are from Outer Space!'

They were just making their funny noses when Minnie's mum came back into the kitchen. She didn't look happy with what she saw.

'I have never ever seen my kitchen in such a mess!'

'I promise we'll clear it up,' said Minnie,

and Minnie's mum went out again.

Maxine looked around her in surprise. 'Our kitchen at home is always like this!' she whispered. 'Your mum is a bit boring!'

'No, she isn't!' said Minnie.

'Doesn't she ever do anything for fun?' asked Maxine. 'Doesn't she ever do anything silly?'

'Yes, of course she does!' said Minnie. She suddenly felt very cross with Maxine.

'When does she?' asked Maxine.

'Well,' said Minnie. 'You know she's going to play the piano for our assembly? Well, she's going to dress up too! As an insect!'

'Really, truly?' said Maxine.

'Really, truly,' said Minnie.

Minnie's mum was not keen on the idea of dressing up. 'Why ever did you go and tell Maxine that I would?' she said.

Minnie wasn't going to tell her why. 'You've got to, Mum! Please! Mrs Dobbs said *everyone* who is taking part in the assembly should dress up.'

'But it's only my fingers that are taking part!' said Minnie's mum.

'We'll just dress up your fingers then!' said Minnie.

Minnie cut out small, floppy, paper butterfly shapes and coloured them with pens. She cut two slits across each butterfly body so that they would fit on to fingers like rings. She made two of them; one for each hand. She showed them to her mum. 'Will you wear them?' she asked. 'Please?'

'Well,' said Minnie's mum, 'I might.'

When Minnie had gone to bed her mum tried on the butterflies. She carefully added some shiny shapes to their wings.

Next morning, all the children arrived at school in their insect costumes. There were three ladybirds and five spiders, but no other insects from Outer Space.

'We'll win!' whispered Maxine to Minnie.

Minnie was glad that she was dressed up for the assembly. She had to stand up and read her poem and she hoped that nobody would know that she was really Minnie. She read:

> *Spiders can be anywhere*
> *Inside, outside, night or day*
> *When you work or when you play*
> *Hanging from treetops, tickling your toes,*
> *In your hankie when you blow your nose.*
> *So beware!*

Everyone laughed and Minnie went a

happy pink as she sat down again to enjoy the rest of the assembly.

Maxine wasn't frightened about reading her poem. She read it in a loud voice:

Do they sneeze?
Do they eat cheese?
Do they have knees?
I wonder about insects.
Do they laugh?
Do they wear a scarf?
Do they look like a giraffe?
I go on wondering about insects.

The other children read and danced and showed things. Then it was time to sing.

Minnie's mum sat down at the piano to play 'All Things Bright And Beautiful'. As she started to play the butterflies on her fingers started to flap. Up and down danced the fingers and flutter, flutter went the butterflies. They were beautiful. The piano played the tune, but nobody sang! They were all watching the butterflies and laughing.

Minnie's mum changed the tune. She added bits to make her hands go right up

and down the piano and even cross over.

When she finished, everybody clapped and shouted for more. Mrs Dobbs stood up and held up her hand for quiet. 'I'm sure that you will all agree that the prize for the best insect costume should go to Mrs Brown!' she said.

'That's Mum!' said Minnie, and she clapped as hard as she could. 'I'm glad,' she told Maxine. 'I'm even more glad than if *we* had won the prize!'

'So am I,' said Maxine. 'Your mum's brilliant!'

4 Pest friends

'What *are* you doing, Minnie?' asked Maxine. Minnie's face was looking funny. She was doing something odd with her mouth. 'It's my tooth,' she said. 'It flaps like a cat-flap when I talk! I hate it!'

'Yuk!' said Maxine. 'Shall I pull it out for you?'

'No!' said Minnie, and she quickly covered her mouth with a hand.

'Let me just have a look,' said Maxine, so Minnie opened her mouth and curled

45

up her top lip so that Maxine could see the flapping tooth.

Suddenly Maxine took hold of the tooth and pulled.

'Ow!' shouted Minnie as Maxine tugged at the tooth and pulled it right out of Minnie's mouth. Minnie felt with her tongue for the hole where the tooth had come from. The hole felt very big and it tasted funny. It was even worse than the flapping tooth. 'You're horrible, Maxthine!' said Minnie.

Maxine laughed. Minnie sounded so funny. Without the tooth she couldn't say the sound 's' properly.

'Try saying "six sizzling sausages",' said Maxine. 'Go on!'

'It'th not funny!' said Minnie. But Maxine thought it

was. She laughed and laughed. Minnie knew that she would sound funny whatever she said, so she stuck her tongue out, picked up her tooth and went.

Minnie found a mirror and looked at herself in it. With her mouth closed she looked the same as usual. Then she smiled and it made her look like a pirate. She knew that everyone would laugh when they saw her, just as Maxine had. More than almost anything, Minnie hated being laughed at. Well, she would just have to not smile and not talk to anyone until she had grown a new tooth.

Minnie wrapped the old tooth in a bit of paper towel and put it in her pocket. She wondered how long the new tooth would take to grow. Maxine would know. But I'm not asking her! thought Minnie. I'm not talking to anyone, even if it takes weeks!

After playtime Maxine and Minnie sat together, but Minnie wouldn't look at Maxine. Maxine said, 'I'm sorry I pulled out your tooth, Min. I was only trying to help!'

But Minnie didn't answer. She just sat there with her mouth shut tight. Maxine tried again, 'And I'm sorry I laughed at you — but you did sound funny!'

Minnie turned to look out of the window. The thing that Maxine hated more than almost anything was to be ignored. 'You're stupid!' she told Minnie, and she moved to an empty table.

Minnie stayed silent all through Mrs Dobbs' morning lessons. She stayed silent and she didn't smile.

Then, at tidying-up time, Mrs Dobbs told them all, 'A photographer will be coming this afternoon to take a class photograph, so please try to keep nice this lunchtime. No muddy games in the playground and no falling over and losing your teeth! We don't want you to look like a class of monsters!'

Minnie knew that she would be the one looking like a monster. She knew that her mother would buy the photograph and put it on the piano at home and she would be laughed at for ever.

Maxine looked towards Minnie. She saw a tear trickle down Minnie's cheek. 'Are you coming to lunch, Min?' she asked.

Minnie still kept her mouth shut but she shook her head.

'Oh, please yourself,' said Maxine, and she went to join the others for lunch.

That lunchtime, Minnie was hungry, but eating would mean opening her mouth, and opening her mouth would

mean being laughed at. But worse than
that, Maxine wasn't her friend any more.
Minnie sat on a wall in the playground
and watched Maxine when she came out
after lunch. Minnie pretended to be busy
pulling petals off daisies, but she secretly
watched Maxine at the same time.

Maxine was whispering to the children

from their class. Then Maxine pointed to
Minnie and they all laughed.

Minnie felt sick. I hate them all, she
thought. And I especially hate Maxine!
Minnie ran and hid in the toilets for the
rest of lunchtime . . .

As the children came back into the

classroom, Mrs Dobbs put a hand on to Minnie's head and asked, 'Are you all right, Minnie? You don't look very happy.' Minnie just nodded. 'And what about the rest of you?' asked Mrs Dobbs. 'You all seem strangely quiet!' They were quiet. Nobody spoke. 'Have you all lost your voices?' asked Mrs Dobbs.

Nobody answered. Minnie looked around her. All the children, even Maxine, were sitting quietly and had their mouths shut tight. They had smiley eyes and Minnie could tell that they were all sharing some secret. Every child in the class knew what the secret was except Minnie! Being outside a secret is even worse than being laughed at, thought Minnie.

'Well,' said Mrs Dobbs. 'I won't complain. It's a nice change to have you all quiet for once!'

A man with a big nose came through the door. 'Ah!' said Mrs Dobbs. 'And here is Mr Cook, the photographer. He will tell you where to stand, and then I hope that you will all smile nicely for the camera!'

When Mrs Dobbs said, 'Smile for the camera,' there were some bursting noises from Maxine. Some of the other children were having trouble keeping their mouths shut too. They must be thinking how silly I'll look when I smile, thought Minnie. Well, I'm not going to!

Mr Cook sorted the children into

different sizes. Minnie sat on the floor in front with the smallest children. Maxine was behind with the big ones on chairs.

'Now,' said Mr Cook. 'Could you all look at the camera? I want you all to say "Cheese!" after I count to three.'

Minnie bent down low and wished that she could magic herself to disappear.

Mr Cook got his camera ready. 'One, two, three!' he said.

'Cheese!' shouted the whole class except Minnie and then Mr Cook dropped his camera.

The look on Mr Cook's face made Mrs Dobbs stand up and turn round to look at her class. Her mouth dropped open and her hands went to her cheeks. Minnie turned to look too, and her mouth opened in surprise. Every child in the class had horrible teeth! They looked the silliest group of children that Minnie had ever seen. They were all worse than her! Much worse! Some of them had used black stuff to make it look as if teeth were missing. Some had cut fangs from the peel of packed lunch oranges. Others had teeth of all sorts of shapes cut from cardboard. Some were green, some purple, and some even spotted and striped.

Minnie opened her mouth wide and laughed. She stood up straight and looked around and laughed at them all. They all laughed too, but they weren't laughing at Minnie. They were all laughing at themselves!

'Will somebody tell me what on earth is going on?' asked Mrs Dobbs. She said it in a cross voice, but her mouth was twitching with wanting to laugh. 'Which one of you monsters thought of this idea?' she asked.

Maxine put up her hand and smiled bright orange fangs at Mrs Dobbs. 'It was my idea,' she said. Minnie suddenly knew what Maxine's plan was and why she had done it. She didn't feel sick any more. Maxine explained to Mrs Dobbs, 'Minnie was unhappy because she lost a tooth and it made her look silly and talk silly. She was even more unhappy when you told us about the photographer coming. I thought if we all had silly teeth it would make her feel better! I did it for a nice surprise for Minnie,' she said.

'Well it wasn't a nice surprise for Mr Cook, was it?' said Mrs Dobbs.

Mr Cook had picked up his camera and it wasn't broken.

'It gave me a bit of a shock,' he said. 'But I think it's great! I take photographs every day of ordinary classes of children. It makes a change to take a photograph of a class of tooth monsters!'

'I just hope that their parents agree!' said Mrs Dobbs. 'We haven't time to clean you all up now.'

So Mrs Dobbs' class had two photographs taken. One had the children with their mouths closed and not smiling. The other had them smiling their horrible teeth.

Most of the parents wanted to buy the smiling teeth picture. Mrs Dobbs had a copy too. She looked at it and laughed.

'You, Maxine Higgins, are a pest!' she said.

'I know,' said Maxine. 'But it was Minnie's fault too. She was the one who lost a tooth. So, we must be pest friends, mustn't we, Min?'

'Yes,' said Minnie.